For Ridley

First published in 2018 by Nosy Crow Ltd
The Crow's Nest, 14 Baden Place, Crosby Row
London SE1 1YW
www.nosycrow.com

ISBN 978 1 78800 264 6

Nosy Crow and associated logos are trademarks and/or
registered trademarks of Nosy Crow Ltd.

A CIP catalogue record for this book
is available from the British Library.

Printed in China
Papers used by Nosy Crow are made from
wood grown in sustainable forests.

10 9 8 7 6 5 4 3 2 1

WHAT DOES AN ANTEATER EAT?

ROSS COLLINS

I'm hungry.

Good morning.
I know this sounds odd,
but do you happen to know
what an anteater eats?

I'm very busy. Don't bother me.

Ah. I see. I'm sorry to have interrupted you.

Hello. I wonder, do you know
what an anteater eats?

Watermelon.

Watermelon? Really?
Are you sure?

Definitely watermelon. Trust me, I'm a melon expert.

I'm not completely convinced.

Excuse me. I don't suppose you know what an anteater eats, do you?

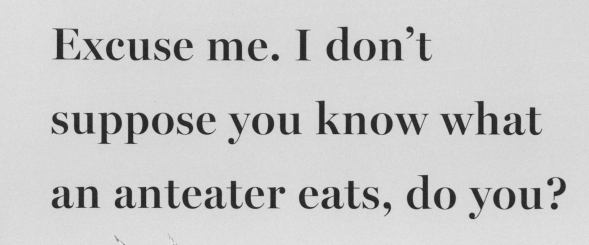

I'm sorry, I don't.
But I would really recommend
that you chew your food.

That's good advice.
Thank you.

Sorry to bother you.
You wouldn't happen to know
what an anteater eats,
would you?

*I'm afraid not. But this old fish
is delicious. Want to try some?*

Thank you, but . . . no.

Hello.

I don't suppose you fellas happen to know what an anteater eats, do you?

I wonder if I might ask . . .
do you happen to know what
an anteater eats?

I'm afraid I don't,
but I must say –
you look very tasty . . .

Oh . . . I really must be going.

Excuse me.

I don't suppose you happen

to know what an . . .

I know what an anteater eats!